The Raven
A Modern Retelling

By Elise Wallace
Illustrated by Linda Silvestri

Publishing Credits

Rachelle Cracchiolo, M.S.Ed., *Publisher*
Conni Medina, M.A.Ed., *Editor in Chief*
Nika Fabienke, Ed.D., *Content Director*
Véronique Bos, *Creative Director*
Shaun N. Bernadou, *Art Director*
Carol Huey-Gatewood, M.A.Ed., *Editor*
Valerie Morales, *Associate Editor*
Kevin Pham, *Graphic Designer*

Image Credits

Illustrated by Linda Silvestri

5301 Oceanus Drive
Huntington Beach, CA 92649-1030
www.tcmpub.com
ISBN 978-1-6449-1323-9

Table of Contents

CHAPTER ONE

The New House

Right away, Heath didn't like the house. Maybe because it was really, really old. His family called it the "new house" because they'd just moved in, but the house must have been built in the 1800s.

His mom talked the house up. She said it had "character." When they first arrived, she pointed excitedly to each room and said, "Look how big!" Heath preferred his room back in California. It was much smaller, but at least it didn't have a weird, mildewy smell.

In this bedroom, there was a giant oak tree outside his window. For some reason, the tree made Heath's stomach turn. Basically, the room gave him the creeps.

Winter in upstate New York was horrible. The skies were gray, and the temperature was frigid. It wasn't until they moved to the East Coast that Heath realized how much he loved life in California. He also desperately missed Lenore, his best friend.

CHAPTER TWO

A Mysterious Dream

The first night in the house, Heath barely slept. Though it didn't seem possible, he was pretty sure his room smelled worse after dark. Also, the house was much noisier at night. Each gust of wind set off a million sounds inside the house: creaks, squeaks, and shudders.

If Heath wasn't fond of the oak tree during the day, he despised it at night. The tree cast a large, spidery shadow across his bedroom floor. In the early hours of the morning, when it was still dark, he dreamed that the tree's shadow grew, stretching across his bedroom walls. The farther the shadow spread, the colder his room became.

In the middle of the dream, the shadow stopped growing. The house became eerily silent. The stillness of the house was so complete that Heath felt like the world had frozen in place. This is when he heard the tapping at his window.

The sound made Heath sit up. He stared at the window from his bed. There was nothing there, just the cold December night and the ominous tree. The sound began again, a quiet but insistent rapping. Something invisible was tapping again and again at his window. Something, he thought, that was eager to get into his room.

Against his better judgement, Heath walked toward the window and opened it. At first, he saw darkness and nothing more. But then, past the giant oak tree, he saw a familiar shape. It was Lenore. She was standing on his front lawn, looking up at Heath and laughing.

He felt the bitter winter air through the open window, and it gave him chills. Lenore had stopped laughing, and her eyes were sad. Heath was about to call her name when he woke up.

CHAPTER THREE

The Next Day

Even though he tried to, Heath couldn't stop thinking about the dream. He thought of the tree's spreading shadow and Lenore's sad expression. He could almost hear the tap-tapping on his bedroom window.

Heath tried to focus on the movers who were walking up and down the driveway. Each time they hauled boxes through the front door, a blast of icy weather whipped through the house. Unfortunately, this made Heath think of the night before, when the house was soundless and frozen.

"We need to get organized," Heath's mom muttered. "I don't want to stumble over boxes for the next year."

"We'll get everything put away," Heath's dad said. "Don't worry!"

His dad hadn't wanted to move, but was hiding it well. Heath's mom had gotten a job at a law firm in Manhattan. Heath guessed she was acting grumpy because she felt guilty about making the family move.

Heath was grumpy, too. He hadn't spoken to Lenore in days. He knew that if they talked, it would make him feel even more miserable about the move. Lenore had sent a flurry of texts when he'd first left, but since then, she'd slowed down. She had sent her latest text earlier that morning. It read:

UM, halloo??

"I'm going back to my room," Heath sighed. "There's nowhere to sit."

But his room wasn't any better. There were more boxes than the day before. Navigating around them was like solving a puzzle—two steps forward, one step back. It took him a full five minutes to make it to his bed.

The text from Lenore had made him smile, but he was still hesitant to text her back. He decided he would get back to her later, once he had something positive to report. More than anything, Heath didn't want to make his best friend sad. He knew that any depressing details about their new house would make Lenore feel awful.

Heath and Lenore met when they were little. They grew up on the same cul-de-sac. Both were *huge* soccer fans. They practiced together constantly and even played on the same teams. Heath and Lenore always competed to see who could get the most goals each season.

Heath's favorite thing about Lenore was that she laughed at anything. She found everything and everyone funny. Lenore laughed at their neighbors, an old couple who would suntan on their front lawn. She giggled at every one of Heath's silly antics. Lenore even laughed at herself.

Heath would never make another friend like Lenore. He was sure of it. Even if he met someone cool at his new school, it wouldn't be the same. Part of him wanted to tell her about his strange dream, but another part of him wanted to push the whole thing out of his head.

Thankfully, he didn't dream about the tree again that night.

CHAPTER FOUR

New Kid

His first day at school wasn't great. It started with the bus ride. Apparently, Heath's house was the very last stop on the school's bus route. There weren't any seats left except for the seat directly behind the bus driver.

Heath felt super awkward sitting at the front of the bus. If Lenore had been sitting next to him, she would have found a way to make him laugh. She would have pretended to be excited to sit behind the bus driver, saying something like, "Maybe if we're very lucky, the bus driver will become our best friend."

Heath had grown up with the same kids his whole life, so starting a new school was strange. At his old school, everyone knew everyone. The kids at the new school seemed regular enough, at least from what he could see of them. They all had on coats, beanies, and scarves. They sort of looked like different versions of the same person.

As soon as Heath reached his classroom, he realized there wasn't anywhere for him to sit. From the look on his new teacher's face, he could tell that she hadn't been expecting him. Heath explained that he was the new student.

The teacher seemed flustered but asked two students to bring in a desk and chair from a nearby classroom. A few of the kids smiled at Heath as he waited, but most of them were busy talking to each other or sneaking looks at their phones. As Heath watched his teacher introduce him to the class, he felt detached from his surroundings. He was trying to put on a brave face, but it was difficult.

I told you, being the new kid sucks. Lenore had warned him. The memory made him smile, despite everything.

CHAPTER FIVE

The Raven

The dream returned that night. It started in the same way, with the tree's shadow growing through the house, darkening every surface it touched. Again, Heath heard a tapping on his bedroom window. This time, he didn't hesitate and moved straight toward the sound.

He didn't see Lenore standing on the lawn, but he did see something, or someone. There was a creature perched on the oak tree's branch closest to the window. It looked like a bird, a very large one. Heath continued to stare at the creature, waiting for his eyes to adjust to the darkness.

The rapping on the window began again. But now, Heath could see that it was the bird making the sound. It stretched forward and tapped against the glass with its beak. Heath could see its eyes, silvery in the moonlight. It was a raven.

There was something unusual about the creature's eyes. The bird was regarding Heath very carefully, as if it were sizing him up. The raven cocked its head to the side and then tapped on the window again.

The bird began to squawk loudly. It was a strange sound, not quite bird-like. The longer Heath listened, the more it didn't sound like the bird was squawking at all, but repeating the same word over and over. He decided to open the window, just a crack. Instantly, cold air filled the room. Heath swallowed and pressed his ear to the opening in the window. "Nevermore, nevermore!" the bird called.

Heath was so shocked to hear the bird speak that he immediately slammed the window shut. The bird, startled by the sound, hopped off the branch and flew away from the oak tree. It was a long time before Heath could catch his breath.

CHAPTER SIX

Awake?

The next morning, Heath wondered if the bird was real or just a dream. And even if the bird was just a figment of his imagination, what on earth did "nevermore" mean? Heath googled the word and was disturbed by the results. According to the dictionary, *nevermore* meant "at no future time; never again."

Heath had a feeling the bird was talking about Lenore. When he'd seen her in the first dream, she had looked sad. Did this mean that he was never going to see Lenore again?

The rest of the day was hazy, and Heath felt like the dream was seeping into his waking hours. During lunch, the strangest thing happened. He was sitting alone, quietly eating his lunch, when he heard Lenore laugh. It was so shocking that Heath immediately stood up and began looking for the source of the sound.

It was a blonde girl who looked just like Lenore. She was still laughing, her head thrown back. Heath stumbled toward the girl, eager to reach his friend. But once he got closer, Heath realized it wasn't Lenore at all. The blonde girl looked at him curiously. Heath shook his head and walked away—was he going crazy?

There was a note waiting for him on the dining table when he arrived home.

Heath, I'll be back in 10 minutes.
Made a quick run to the grocery store.
He set the note down and collapsed on the living room couch. The boxes were finally dwindling, and there were just a few scattered throughout the house.

He was completely exhausted. He was about to nod off when he heard the sound again—the bird's tapping. Heath jumped from the couch and dashed up the stairs leading to his bedroom. With each step he took, the tapping continued, becoming progressively louder and louder. The sound stopped when he opened his bedroom door.

Heath stared at the oak tree's bare branches and waited patiently. Then, the sound started again. It was a huge noise, one that reverberated through the entire house. Somehow, Heath knew it was coming from the front door.

By the time he reached the front door, the house was actually shaking from the noise. It sounded like a giant was trying to punch his way inside the house. Heath reached the doorknob and turned it.

Suddenly, he was back in California, and he and Lenore were stretched out on her front lawn, staring up at a cloudless sky. Lenore was talking about their last game, complaining about one of the calls the referee had made. Heath tried to respond, but his mouth wouldn't open. Lenore's eyes opened wide—she was scared.

Then, just as quickly, California and Lenore faded. Heath was back in bed, with the raven perched on his chest.

"Where is Lenore?" Heath shouted at the raven.

"Nevermore," the bird squawked.

CHAPTER SEVEN

Lenore at Last

When Heath woke on the living room couch, he felt like he'd been sleeping for days. The sky outside, which had been a gloomy charcoal gray since they'd first arrived, was nearly blue. Despite his horrible nightmare, Heath felt lighter than he had in a very long time. He had to text Lenore and find out if she was alright.

But when he reached for his phone, there were already five texts waiting. They were all from Lenore.

Check your phone!!

I've texted u 1000 times!!

Just bc ur in New York doesn't mean we have 2 stop talking.

I have great news...

News that maybe involves me and a flight out there!!

Heath read and reread Lenore's messages. She was coming to visit! He couldn't believe he was going to see his best friend again. The raven and his mysterious nightmares had been wrong. He sighed, flooded with relief. Heath couldn't wait to tell Lenore everything.

About Us

The Author

Elise Wallace is a children's book author and editor. She has written about everything from sled dog racing in Alaska to the wonder of Día de los Muertos. This book was inspired by Edgar Allan Poe's "The Raven," which was written in 1845. In his poem, the narrator is mourning his lost love, Lenore, when he encounters the raven. Poe's narrator asks the bird again and again about Lenore. Each time, the bird simply responds, "Nevermore."

The Illustrator

Linda Silvestri is an illustrator and graphic designer in Southern California. Her whimsical creations have found their way into editorial, advertising, and children's markets. When she isn't prying one of three cats from her drawing board, you can find her working out of the home she shares with her husband, Tom